AR ATOS B.L. 3.3
ATOS Points 0.5

STARRING MIRETTE & BELLINI

Emily Arnold McCully

G.P. PUTNAM'S SONS · NEW YORK

For Sarah and David Pagels

The artwork for this book was created with watercolors and pastels on Arcnes paper.

Copyright © 1997 by Emily Arnold McCully. All rights reserved. This book, or parts thereof, may not be reproduced in any form without permission in writing from the publisher. G. P. Putnam's Sons, a division of The Putnam & Grosset Group, 200 Madison Avenue, New York, NY 10016. G. P. Putnam's Sons, Reg. U.S. Pat. & Tm. Off. Published simultaneously in Canada. Printed in Hong Kong by South China Printing Co. (1988) Ltd. Lettering by David Gatti. Text set in Goudy Old Style.
Library of Congress Cataloging-in-Publication Data. McCully, Emily Arnold. Starring Mirette and Bellini / written and illustrated by Emily Arnold McCully. p. cm. Summary: After the Great Bellini teaches young Mirette to walk the high wire, she uses her talent to free him from prison, and both resolve to help others become free. [1. Aerialists—Fiction. 2. Tightrope walking—Fiction. 3. Freedom—Fiction.] I. Title. PZ7.M47815Ml 1997 [E]—dc20 95-34115 CIP AC ISBN 0-399-22636-2
3 5 7 9 10 8 6 4

All of Paris was talking: Young Mirette had walked on the high wire with the Great Bellini.

Bellini had invited Mirette to become his partner. "I will teach you everything I know. We must trust each other completely," he said. "We will live our lives on the wire."

They practiced on a low wire. Mirette learned to cross without raising her arms for balance. She learned to feel the weight of every suspended part of her body and then to forget it. She learned to be utterly still, except for her feet, carrying her along above the ground.

Then Bellini taught her to balance on his shoulders and to do cartwheels.

When she had mastered these feats on the low wire, they rehearsed on a wire forty feet above the ground. Mirette never thought of the danger. She was free, surrounded by air!

"We are ready to perform!" Bellini declared at last.

Bellini arranged for a grand tour of the great cities of Europe. In Milan, they sipped tea at a table high over a square.

In Budapest, Mirette jumped through a paper hoop.

In Vienna, she and Bellini walked from opposite ends of the wire and passed without touching!

For their grand finale, they returned to Paris, where Bellini staged a walk at the Eiffel Tower. They performed somersaults backwards. Paris celebrated with a parade.

Still they practiced.

One morning, Bellini said to Mirette, "I have shown you everything I know except the Death Walk. One walks up an inclined wire, blindfolded. Very few people have done it. This is so difficult, it is always announced as an 'attempt.'"

"Teach me," Mirette responded.

Finding her way without eyes was a torment. The wire seemed never to be still. Gripping with her toes was agonizing.

"You must have patience as well as discipline to succeed," Bellini said. "One day you will do it."

Then a cable arrived from Russia. Mirette and Bellini were invited to perform in St. Petersburg.

"This is a great honor," Bellini told Mirette. "I studied there as a young man. The Imperial Ballet and the circus are the greatest in the world."

"We must go!" Mirette laughed. "I think I will see the whole world from our wire."

As they traveled toward Russia by train, Mirette asked Bellini what they would perform.

Bellini said, "We will cross the frozen Neva River. No one has done it. It will be beautiful, a perfect salute to the city."

In the morning, as they passed a village, Mirette saw a ragged band of people. "Who are they?" she asked. "They look starved!"

"They are the poor people of Russia," Bellini explained. "There is not enough food, and some of them have no homes of their own. The country is ruled by a czar who pays little attention to them."

The train moved on, but Mirette could not forget those faces.

In the distance, the sun shone on the gold and painted roofs of St. Petersburg. How rich the city looked.

At the station, a woman pushed her way through the crowds. "Vera!" Bellini cried as they embraced. "This is Mirette."

The woman smiled. "We were students together," she said. "You will be my guests while you are here."

That night Mirette listened as the old friends recalled their student days and talked of hard times in Russia, of hunger and hopelessness.

"When anyone tries to speak out or to change things, the czar's police take him away to jail."

"But this is terrible!" cried Mirette. "Can't we do something?"

"Maybe you can," Vera said.

"Tell us," Bellini urged her.

"When you and Mirette are above the river, speak to the people. Tell them from the wire that you believe in freedom and come from a city where the people *are* free."

"We will!" Bellini declared.

On the day of the walk, people gathered along the frozen river. Bellini walked to the center of the wire with Mirette on his shoulders. The crowd roared.

Mirette heard only the singing of the wire. Bellini lifted her with one arm, turned full circle, set her down, and knelt as she ran to the end.

Bellini followed and they stood together. Mirette had never felt so free.

Bellini spoke: "One day, you too will be free! Do not lose hope!" A great cheer rose up from the people.

When they came down, they were surrounded by exultant people. But suddenly, soldiers broke through and carried Bellini away. Mirette cried out. A soldier pushed her to the ground.

Mirette was afraid for the first time in her life. She looked up at the faces of strangers in a place far from home. But Vera was there. "Come, child. We must go home."

"But Bellini!" Mirette said.

"We will try to help him," Vera told her.

That night there was a meeting. "We have a friend inside the jail who knows where Bellini is," a man said.

"We must rescue him!" Mirette cried.

"There is no way to reach him. Soldiers are posted everywhere."

"His window looks out the back, over the canal. They can't patrol there."

"But how can we get to him?"

"I think I know a way," Mirette said. "It is a feat I have never performed. But I practiced it blindfolded, so I could do it in the dark."

"Do you mean walk a wire to his window? But how would we attach it?"

"Bellini has told me that a wire can be shot a long way with a crossbow. Can you get one?"

Vera's eyes glowed. "Of course."

Mirette spent the next day by herself. She couldn't practice the feat, so she went over and over it in her mind. That night, she and Vera and two strong men went to a spot on the canal across from Bellini's window. He had been told what to expect by their friend inside the prison.

Mirette tied a small hacksaw to her belt. The men attached the wire to the crossbow. They took careful aim and fired. The wire held. Bellini must have secured it to the window bars. The rest was up to Mirette.

"I will now attempt the Death Walk," she said to herself. The night was as black as any blindfold. Mirette inched forward, thinking only of the wire. She couldn't look down, couldn't look back. How long had she been climbing? It seemed forever. . . .

Mirette saw a hand reach out of the darkness. It was Bellini's. She climbed onto the windowsill. Bellini took the hacksaw. A wagon rumbled over the cobblestones as he began to cut the bars. She clung to the ledge.

"It's done," Bellini whispered at last. He squeezed through the hole he had made and stood beside her. "I'll follow you, brave Mirette. . . ."

They inched blindly downward. Water lapped at the sides of the canal. Soon they could hear guards pacing in the street. Vera and her friends were beckoning shadows. At last they touched ground. They had done it!

"Now we must get you to the border!" Vera said.

Safely back in Paris, Mirette asked Bellini, "Will they ever be free?"

"Maybe not soon, but one day," he said. "Freedom can't be stopped forever."

"And we must keep walking the wire and showing people that everything is possible!" Mirette exclaimed.

"Yes," Bellini agreed. "And now something has come to us from America: an invitation to us both to cross Niagara Falls. Shall we go . . .?"